You do not need to read this page –
just get on with the book!

First published in 2005 in Great Britain by
Barrington Stoke Ltd, Sandeman House, Trunk's Close,
55 High Street, Edinburgh EH1 1SR
www.barringtonstoke.co.uk

ISBN 1-842993-19-4

Printed in Great Britain by Bell & Bain Ltd

MEET THE AUTHOR – HILARY McKAY

What is your favourite animal?
Fox
What is your favourite boy's name?
Jim
What is your favourite girl's name?
Bella
What is your favourite food?
Apples
What is your favourite music?
Classic rock and Bach
What is your favourite hobby?
Natural history

MEET THE ILLUSTRATOR – KIRSTIN HOLBROW

What is your favourite animal?
My dog, Pewter Plum
What is your favourite boy's name?
George
What is your favourite girl's name?
Beryl
What is your favourite food?
Shellfish
What is your favourite music?
Ambient techno
What is your favourite hobby?
Rowing on the river Wye

For Emily and Bella

Contents

Chapter 1
Emily and Tom

Emily lived with her grandma and her twin brother Tom and a wicked old lady called Aunty Bess. They had a little house just outside the town. A road went past their garden gate and on down to the sea.

Emily and Tom had never seen the sea. They had never seen the town either. They never went anywhere except round the corner to school. Wicked old Aunty Bess would not let them.

Wicked old Aunty Bess was the boss in their house.

Emily and Tom's grandma never said anything to anyone. All day long she sat outside in a rocking chair by the door of the little house, gazing at the three apple trees that grew in the garden. When it was sunny she sat in the sun. When it was raining she sat under a huge umbrella. The only sound she made was the tiny creak of the rocking chair.

Emily and Tom had no toys or books or pets.

"Toys and books and pets are for good children!" said wicked old Aunty Bess. "Birthdays and Christmas and friends round to play are for good children too! So squish squash! None for you!"

She was not fair. Emily looked at her and thought, *Squish squash to you!*

Tom looked at Aunty Bess and thought, *How bad are we?*

We are not that bad, thought Tom.

What was good in Tom and Emily's life was the road that went past their garden gate. Luckily for Emily and Tom, a great many interesting people went along that road. They were going to the sea from the town, or else to the town from the sea. Every day Emily and Tom watched them go past.

Chapter 2
The Gypsy

One day Emily and Tom saw a lovely gypsy-man go past. He had gold earrings and a red shirt and black twinkling eyes. He wore high boots with heels that clacked, and he strode along with his hands in his pockets. He was whistling a tune so bright and clear that it rocked up to the tops of the apple trees.

Emily heard the gypsy coming from far away. She ran to the fence and there he was. He was leading a small grey donkey.

Emily's best thing to do was swopping.

Emily was a wild and exciting swopper.

The gypsy seemed to know this without being told. He looked over the fence at Emily, and he said, "It's a shining day, it's a lovely day! It's a lovely day for a swop!"

"Yes," said Emily, nodding her head.

"Yes," said the gypsy, and he leaned on the fence and crossed his long legs and whistled a bit more of his tune. Then he said, "So? Fancy a donkey?"

Emily nodded even harder.

The gypsy looked around the garden. There was nothing in it but the apple trees, and Tom, and the silent little grandma, rocking to and fro in her chair.

"You could never carry the apple trees away," said Emily. "And I'm keeping Tom!"

"What about the old lady?" asked the gypsy. "She looks a nice, quiet old lady. I could just do with one like that."

He looked at Emily and gave her a wink. Emily winked back and nodded again.

Then all in a flash the donkey was in the garden, and Emily and Tom's grandma was being jumped over the fence by the lovely gypsy. And then both of them were gone.

That was Emily's most exciting swop ever. She was only six years old and she did it all by herself with her thumb in her mouth.

"Emily!" shouted wicked old Aunty Bess, when she found out what Emily had done. "Are you standing there telling me you went and swopped your grandma for a donkey?"

"Yes, Aunty Bess," said Emily, with her thumb still in her mouth. "That's what I did. Didn't I, Tom?"

"Yes, Aunty Bess," said Tom.

"Tom!" shouted wicked old Aunty Bess, even more crossly. "Are you standing there telling me you WATCHED EMILY DO IT?"

"Yes, Aunty Bess," said Tom. "We thought it was a good swop. We hoped you would be glad."

Aunty Bess was not glad at all. She moaned and moaned. She was a great moaner. She said the donkey would have to go. The donkey took no notice. It stayed. It lived in the garden under the apple trees and Emily and Tom loved it more than all the toys and books and pets in the world.

"Don't ever let me catch you chatting with gypsies again!" growled Aunty Bess, when she gave Emily and Tom their supper of dry bread and water. "IF he was a gypsy, WHICH I don't believe! He sounds more like a PIRATE to me!"

"We won't let you catch us, Aunty Bess," promised Emily and Tom. But every day they watched over the fence, hoping for another lovely gypsy to come whistling down the road.

Chapter 3

The Spanish Lady and the Man with Owls on his Shoulders

Emily and Tom did not see their gypsy again for a long, long time.

They stayed in the little house, and nothing much happened until they were nearly ten years old. By then the donkey was very fat, and they were very thin. Wicked old Aunty Bess had stopped giving

them bread with their water for supper, and she had stopped giving them water with their bread for breakfast. Luckily they had a secret store of apples from the apple trees in the garden, and on school days they had school dinners. Emily and Tom thought school dinners were wonderful. Nobody else in the school thought school dinners were wonderful, but nobody else had to live with wicked old Aunty Bess.

By the time Emily was nearly ten she hardly sucked her thumb at all, but her swopping was wilder than ever.

A Spanish lady with red and orange skirts and high-heeled shoes came tapping along the road. Ever since the gypsy went away Emily had been teaching herself to whistle his tune. By now she could whistle so loud and so high the notes went bright and clear up to the tops of the apple trees. Emily swopped the tune with the Spanish lady and got a wailing violin. She wanted the violin for Tom. He loved tunes as much as she did, but he could never learn how to whistle.

Very soon after Tom got his violin a tall thin man with an owl on each shoulder came by. He swopped a violin book for a bag of fallen apples.

It was a very good book to learn from. Tom soon learnt to play his violin. But the music made wicked old Aunty Bess very cross indeed. She didn't believe Emily and Tom when they told her about the Spanish lady and the tall thin man with owls on his shoulders. She spat on the ground and she said, "Arr! Squish squash! I never heard such lies! They sound exactly like PIRATES to me!"

"Oh," said Emily and smiled. She was beginning to think a lot about pirates.

Wicked old Aunty Bess did not let Tom play his violin in the house. He had to play in the garden and the noise made every dog that lived between the town and the sea sit down and howl like a wolf. Emily and Tom loved to listen to the dogs. They used to try and guess what they looked like. They still had never seen the sea, or gone into the town.

When they asked if they could do these things wicked old Aunty Bess said, "Just you try and I'll roast you and eat you! And then I'll use your bones to light the fire."

Emily and Tom did not think she really would use their bones to light the fire. They did not think she could light the fire. She always made them do it. But they did believe she would eat them. Wicked old Aunty Bess ate anything. With their own eyes they had seen her munch up a cat that was struck by

lightning and fell dead down the chimney.
So they did not try to run away.

Chapter 4
The Sailor

It was hard for Emily and Tom never to have any birthday presents. It was very bad when they were ten. At school everyone thought ten was a very exciting age to be.

"Ten is special!" people said, and had loads of presents and extra good parties. They did not ask Emily and Tom to come to the parties because everyone knew they never went anywhere. Anyway, Emily and Tom had no clothes except the ragged old things they wore to school. They had nothing they could wear to birthday parties.

"I don't care," said Emily, but Tom knew she did care. For their tenth birthday he made her a beautiful necklace out of silver grass and some pearly beads he found in the mud at the back of the house. Tom was a kind, hard-working boy. He was very good at making things.

Emily was not good at making things. She was not hard-working either. This did not matter a bit because she was so fantastic at swopping.

For Tom's tenth birthday present she swopped her own long gold curls for a tiny spotty kitten. He had a soft round face and tufty red fur on his shoulders.

Emily did not like her curls much. They were always getting tangled up when she climbed the apple trees. One day she cut them off and hung them over the fence just as a sailor came rolling down the road. The sailor had baggy white trousers and blue tattoos all over his arms. When he saw Emily's curls hanging on the fence he told Emily they were exactly what he needed to fix the rigging on his ship.

"What's rigging?" asked Emily, and the sailor kindly told her all about ropes and sails and flags and knots and anchors. Wicked old Aunty Bess came home and found him still talking to Emily. Aunty Bess was very rude to him. She said to Emily, "What did I tell you about chatting with gypsies?"

The sailor was very polite. He said, "I am not a gypsy, madam. I'm a blue water sailor from over the seven seas."

"Squish squash, as if I cared!" snapped Aunty Bess. "You look more like a PIRATE to me!"

"Thank you, madam," said the sailor, and he looked very happy and he bowed very low. Emily knew then that a pirate was a wonderful thing to be.

Chapter 5
The Silver Woman

Tom was very happy with his little spotty kitten. Wicked old Aunty Bess was not. She said, "I shall drown it in a bucket."

She might as well have tried to drown the moon in a bucket. When the kitten was awake it moved as fast as magic, and when it was asleep it curled up on the little donkey's back. Wicked old Aunty Bess was not able to get near the donkey. It kicked anyone it didn't like, and its hooves were as hard as stones.

The little spotty kitten grew and grew. They called it Spotty.

"How lucky that Spotty loves bread and water and apple cores so much," said Tom. "He's very strong and healthy. I think he's bigger than a normal cat. He's bigger than the one that fell down the chimney anyway."

"Yes," agreed Emily. Then they both stroked Spotty who purred like a bagful of thunder and stood on his back paws and put his front paws kindly on their shoulders.

"His spots are shaped like roses!" said Tom. "I think he is a special sort of cat. I shall look him up in a book at school."

"Stop fussing over that horrid cat and come and cut my toenails!" called wicked old

Aunty Bess out of the window. "And then you can rub my back and cook my supper! And bring me another bottle of beer! I feel like being looked after tonight!"

Looking after wicked old Aunty Bess was very hard work. By the time she was safely drunk in bed for the night, Emily and Tom were very tired.

Tom sat on the steps and played long slow notes on his violin. Spotty climbed onto the very top of the roof. He lay with two paws dangling down on each side and his tail curled up around the chimney. All the dogs between the town and the sea howled, loud enough to drag down the moon. Emily hummed the gypsy's tune to the donkey until it went to sleep, and then she went and leaned on the fence.

Down the road came a thin silver woman. She moved with a sound like wind.

As she came closer Emily saw that she was a little bit see-through, like cloudy glass.

"Are you a ghost?" asked Emily, trying to be brave.

"Oh no," said the silver woman. "I just came because I heard the music."

Then she looked hard at Emily's necklace of silver grass and pearly beads, and asked, "What would you swop for that?"

All at once, Spotty stood up on the roof. He looked huge with the starry sky behind him. The donkey opened its eyes and stamped his hooves. All the dogs stopped howling.

Emily held her necklace tight with both hands. "I won't swop this," she said. "Not for anything in the world."

"Good girl," said the silver woman. "That was the right answer."

Spotty lay down again and the donkey stood still and all the dogs began to howl once more. From under her cloak, the silver woman took out a basket of carrots, three long loaves of bread and a pot of honey. Then she swopped them all for a drink of water.

So that night Emily and Tom and Spotty and the donkey had supper under the apple trees.

Wicked old Aunty Bess was fast asleep. She never knew anything about it.

"What a lovely silver woman," said Tom, full of bread and honey for the first time in his life.

"Yes," nodded Emily, and then she laughed and said sleepily, "I expect Aunty Bess would tell us she was a pirate."

Chapter 6
Spotty

The last peaceful time Emily and Tom had at the little house was the night the silver woman came and gave them bread and honey, and carrots for the donkey.

Tom did not forget his plan to find out more about Spotty in a book at school. He liked looking things up in books. He started the very next day. First he looked in a book called *Pet Cats and How to Care for Them.*

There were no cats like Spotty in that book.

Then he looked in a book called *Pet Cats and Cats in the Wild.*

There were no cats like Spotty in that book either.

Then he found another book. It had a very short title. *Big Cats.*

"Don't look in that book!" begged Emily. She was starting to feel very worried about what Tom might find out. "What does it matter what Spotty is?" she went on. "Let's just love him like we always have!"

"All right," said Tom, because he could see she was upset, and he closed the book.

That night they went home to love Spotty just like they always had. Spotty was asleep in the middle of the roof of the little house.

And the roof was sagging. It was curved like a washing line, with too much washing on it. When Spotty saw Emily and Tom looking at him he yowled because he was so glad to see them. And then he stood up and stretched. He stretched his front paws forward as far as they would go, and he could just touch the round chimney at one end of the roof. Then he stretched his back paws backwards as far as they would go, and he could just touch the square chimney at the other end of the roof.

Then Spotty danced about on the top of the house and the roof bent lower and lower.

Emily and Tom always slept in the attic on piles of grass they picked in the garden.

That night when they lay down on their little grass beds, they saw that the roof was sagging so low in the middle that it almost touched their noses.

"I *must* find out more about Spotty!" whispered Tom.

"Yes, I think you better had," agreed Emily.

The picture in *Big Cats* that looked most like Spotty was of a leopard. The leopard had rose shaped spots, just like Spotty. It had enormous padding paws, with enormous curving claws, just like Spotty. The book called *Big Cats* said that of all the big cats there were, leopards were the most dangerous and wild.

"Oh, Emily!" said Tom. "Aunty Bess will never let Spotty stay if he's a leopard!"

"Don't let's tell her," said Emily.

"But Spotty might eat her!"

"What if he does?" said Emily.

Tom did not like Aunty Bess either, but he did not think Spotty should eat her. He did not think Spotty should eat anybody and he told Emily so.

"No," Emily said. "But if Spotty had to eat *one* person, one person in the whole world, who would you pick?"

"Aunty Bess," Tom said at last.

"And," said Emily, "Spotty might not be a leopard at all. He isn't exactly like the picture of the leopard in the book."

Ben looked at the picture again and said, "His paws are!"

"The one in the book," said Emily, "didn't have wings."

Tom looked at Emily. Then he looked at Spotty. Then he looked at Emily again. She was right. The tufts on Spotty's back had grown. And the next day he looked up Spotty in a book called *Most Dangerous Magic Beasts.*

"He's a rare sort of griffin," he whispered to Emily in bed that night, and wicked old Aunty Bess, who had been listening through a rat hole, heard him.

"A griffin!" she yelled. She was mad with anger. "A griffin! Only a PIRATE would give a child a griffin for a pet!"

"Do you think she's right?" whispered Tom.

"I hope so," whispered Emily.

Chapter 7
Grandma

The next morning wicked old Aunty Bess said she knew she should have drowned Spotty in a bucket when they'd first got him.

When Spotty heard that, he spat and growled and showed his teeth and claws.

"He's not safe," said wicked old Aunty Bess.

"Don't worry," said Tom. "We won't let him hurt you."

"What will I do when you're at school?" asked Aunty Bess. "What will he do then? Well, you'll just have to stay at home!"

Emily and Tom went white with horror. No school meant no school dinners. They would only have bread and water and apples to eat.

"Children have to go to school, Aunty Bess," said Emily. "It's the law."

"We'll see about that!" said Aunty Bess, and she wrote a note which said,

Dear School,

Emily and Tom will not be coming to school any more.

They have to stay home to make sure their pet griffin does not eat me.

Yours truly,
A. Bess

P.S. So you can cancel their school dinners.

School sent a note back straight away saying,

That's cool.
Love school.
P.S. We have cancelled their school dinners.

"So ha, ha! Squish squash!" said Aunty Bess. She waved the school's letter over her head. "Told you so!"

Emily wanted to run away.

Tom did not. Sometimes he thought Emily was too brave. But he did not say that, because he liked her the way she was. And, anyway, he was not sure if he was right.

Perhaps nobody could be too brave.

Perhaps he was not brave enough. He said, "Aunty Bess said she would eat us if we tried to run away."

So they stayed, and they were very hungry. And as they got hungrier, Spotty grew fiercer. He got so fierce that he scared the donkey, even though they had always been friends.

One night the donkey was so jumpy and jittery he did a very foolish thing.

He chewed all the bark off the apple trees.

If trees lose their bark it kills them.

The apple trees died.

"We *must* run away," said Emily. "There will only be bread and water to eat now. Don't be frightened of Aunty Bess. I am sure she won't eat us. Spotty wouldn't let her."

"No," agreed Tom. "I don't think he would. But poor Aunty Bess! She would feel so lonely!"

Sometimes Emily thought Tom was too kind. But she did not say that, because she liked him the way he was. And, anyway, she was not sure if she was right.

Perhaps nobody could be too kind. Perhaps she was not kind enough.

So they stayed. And they were very, very hungry. And they were quite unhappy too.

Then, just when they thought things could not get worse, Emily and Tom heard someone singing along the road. Crackly, screechy, squawky singing. And they ran to the fence just in time to see a little old lady jump right over it. Grandma.

Grandma had come back, and she had changed a lot. They didn't know where she had been, but she must have had a very good time there. She smoked a big pipe, and she sang rude songs. She danced strange clattering dances on the kitchen floor. She whirled a big rope round her head like a lasso and got the rocking chair.

"She's bonkers!" said Emily.

The moment wicked old Aunty Bess and Grandma saw each other they started to argue. They shouted and banged, and Grandma tried to catch Aunty Bess with the rope.

"Ha, ha! Missed again!" shouted wicked old Aunty Bess. "Squish squash! You always will! I'm the boss in this house!"

Then Grandma and wicked old Aunty Bess chased each other round and round the dead apples trees, and all through the house, and onto the sagging roof and off again.

They looked like they were having a very good time. But the noise was dreadful.

Tom couldn't hear his violin when he played it. The dogs that lived between the town and the sea couldn't hear themselves howl. And Spotty spat and hissed on the roof, while the donkey eeyored in the garden.

"Tom," said Emily, very firmly, "*now* we must run away! Grandma will stop Aunty Bess from being lonely. And Spotty will stop her eating us."

So they did.

They ran away.

They jumped over the fence and ran down the road that led to the sea. Tom took his violin, and Emily carried his violin book, and Spotty and the donkey ran after them.

Chapter 8
The Pirate

Emily and Tom ran and ran. They ran away from wicked Aunty Bess and Grandma and the little house by the road. And when they got too tired to run, they walked. And when they were too tired to walk, the donkey carried Emily and Spotty carried Tom.

And at last they saw the sea.

When at last they saw the sea, the enormous, silver, shining sea, Emily and Tom slid off the donkey and Spotty. They gazed and gazed and gazed. For a long time they said nothing at all, because it was so beautiful. And then at last Tom said, "We should have run away ages ago."

But Emily shook her head and answered, "No. It wouldn't have been kind."

And then they walked slowly down to the edge of the sea.

Waiting there was a ship. A sailing ship, green and gold with two tall masts. It was rocking gently on the tide. The rolled-up sails were red and white striped. The flags that blew above the sails were black as night. At the front of the ship, the prow was carved like a golden griffin. On the decks were piles of apple barrels and stacks of hay. A long bendy plank stretched from the ship to the harbour, and at the end of the plank stood A PIRATE!

They knew he was a pirate because he had a black hat with a snow white feather. He had gold teeth that sparkled in his smile, and sea-blue eyes, and a spyglass and a sharp, steel cutlass. On his shoulder was a parrot.

When the pirate saw Emily and Tom, he took off his hat with a great sweep and tossed it high in the air, and he shouted, "HERE YOU ARE AT LAST!"

And at the sound of his voice, a crowd of people came up onto the deck. The gypsy, and the sailor, the Spanish lady and the man with owls on his shoulder, and last of all, the silver woman. They rushed Emily and Tom

on board the ship. Then they crowded round asking questions.

"Was the donkey useful?" asked the gypsy.

"Oh yes," said Emily. "Thank you very much. He saved Spotty from being drowned in a bucket!"

"And what about the violin?" said the Spanish lady.

"It was just what I needed," said Tom. "Because I've tried and tried but I really can't whistle."

"And the book?" asked the man with the owls.

"I couldn't have ever learnt to play the violin without the book," said Tom.

"And what about Spotty?" asked the sailor.

"Spotty has been wonderful!" said Emily. "I think he saved us from being eaten! And look how big he has grown!"

"And did you like the bread and honey?" asked the silver woman.

"Very, very, very much," said Emily and Tom.

"I am sorry about Grandma," the gypsy told them. "I had to let her go. She was the noisiest old lady I ever swopped for a donkey!"

"I think she'll be perfect company for Aunty Bess," said Tom.

"Now," said the pirate, handing the parrot to Emily and the spyglass to Tom, "the tide is turning! Will you sail along with us? What do you think? Will you swop a life ashore to sail the seven seas?"

He put his hands on his hips and looked down at Emily and Tom.

"Yes, yes!" shouted Tom at once.

"And what about you?" the pirate asked Emily, and he winked, waiting for an answer.

Emily had known for a long, long time that a pirate was a wonderful thing to be. So she winked back at the pirate and nodded and smiled.

That is the end. They sailed away with the pirate, and Spotty and the donkey and all the friends who had looked after them so well, and they lived happily ever after.

And Grandma lived happily ever after too.

And so did wicked old Aunty Bess.

They mended the roof and planted more apple trees and took turns with the rope and the rocking chair.

Sometimes, on stormy nights, Emily and Tom would hear their voices, blown on the wind, from far away.

"Ha ha! Squish squash! Missed again!"

And terrible screechy singing.

And all the dogs howling between the town and the sea.